Finding Fatima

Finding Fatima

J. W. Hoffman

Copyright © 2015 J. W. Hoffman
All rights reserved.

ISBN: 1532801831
ISBN 13: 9781532801839
Library of Congress Control Number: 2016906475
CreateSpace Independent Publishing Platform
North Charleston, South Carolina

I would like to dedicate this book to my entire family for their support.

I would also like to thank my husband, family, and friends for always pushing me and believing in me no matter what. I am blessed to have an understanding husband and four wonderful gifts I call my children.

I also would like to send a warm salute to my students past and present.

This book combines two of my favorite literary loves: my poetry and fictional writing. Happy reading!

Disclaimer

This is a work of fiction. Names, characters, businesses, places, events, and incidents are either the products of the author's imagination or used in a fictitious manner. Any resemblance to actual persons, living or dead, or actual events is purely coincidental.

Table of Contents

Acknowledgments · xi
Preface · xiii
Prologue · xv
The Intro · xvii

Chapter 1   Searching · 1
Chapter 2   Say What? · 5
Chapter 3   The Loner · 7
Chapter 4   The New Me · 10
Chapter 5   Justifiable Injustice · 12
Chapter 6   Love · 20
Chapter 7   Say My Name · 28
Chapter 8   My Girls · 31
Chapter 9   Celebration · 36
Chapter 10   Big Girls Don't Cry · 43
Chapter 11   Day by Day · 48
Chapter 12   Liberty · 52
Chapter 13   Lips · 59
Chapter 14   The Blues · 62
Chapter 15   Saying Good-bye · 66

Epilogue Just Me · 71

Acknowledgments

I would first like to take the time to thank God for allowing me to actually finish a task that I started years ago. I am also grateful for the support of my loved ones, my patient and wonderful husband, my children, my beautiful mother, blessed siblings, and all of my family and friends.

I love you all!

Preface

My Reality

*My reality lies inside of me
It is the force that controls
The type of person I let the outside see
Your reality is your perception of what I should be
Oftentimes shattered by who I am
How can you judge for me what is real or fake?
Why assume that you are the keeper of
my soul or the master of my fate?
Reality in itself can be bleak
Without substantial faith to sustain us we are weak
Just because I see flowers and you view thorns
Does not mean one of us has to change what we see
For after all
this world that I must live in
is my Reality*

—J. W. Hoffman

Prologue

OK, I can't believe I am doing this at all, but if I don't write out the feelings and emotions I have inside, sometimes I feel like I am going to go crazy, or I feel like I am going to explode. People think that poetry is about love and all that mushy crap, but my poetry is different. My poetry helps me express whatever is going on in my life, even if it happens to SUCK! Yes, I said it, MY LIFE SUCKS! I mean think about it, I am an awkward 14-year- old- girl with no friends and no social life. My only real companion is my love for food, food is comforting, it's delicious, and it makes me happy when I am sad. The only problem I have with food is that when you eat too much of it, it happens to show on the outside.

The Intro

Sometimes I stare at my reflection in the mirror, and I just stand there and ask the same questions. Who am I? Why am I here? What's my purpose? Well, if people were being nice, they would call me mixed, biracial, or black/white. The not-so-nice ones would call me a half breed, zebra, Oreo, or the old school term: mulatto. I think *mulatto* is a cool word, kind of like gelato. Anyway, I prefer to be called by my name. I am Fatima.

Like all kids born every day in this crazy world, I didn't ask to be born. I have my parents to thank for that. They fell madly in love one day, got married, and two years later I was born. My parents are perfect for each other, and they are embarrassingly affectionate all the time. I guess I should be happy. Life could be a lot worse. I could have been a nonexistent blank ball of emptiness, a still-born kid, an aborted kid, a homeless poor kid, a third-world-country kid—the list goes on. I'm not any of those things. Instead I'm a black/white kid, and I don't have a clue where I fit in.

The funny thing is sometimes I feel that I do. I mean, I am all those people or all those things. I get so depressed some times. I keep trying to find my place, like where I fit in this crazy world. Then at other times, I rebel, because who wants to fit in with a bunch of clone-like, plastic, superficial, fickle idiots? Not me. Definitely not me.

Chapter 1

Searching

Who Am I?

*I'm on a quest, a search, a destination
At least I hope I am
I'm trying to find me
Out of the millions of people that I see
I'm hoping to be unique
I want to be special
Set apart from the norm
I have one question though
"God,
Where do I belong?"*

—Fatima

J. W. Hoffman

OK, the background on me is pretty simple. I, like hundreds of kids in America was born to one African American parent and one Caucasian parent. Back in the day, if I was born during slavery, I would be considered black just because I had a drop of black blood in my body, even if I could probably "pass" for white as some slaves did.

Then again, because I have a white mom, I'm pretty much considered white among her family and group of friends. Whenever we are around my mom's side of the family, they just pretend like we are all the same color.

I remember we were all at Virginia Beach, and I was hanging out with my cousins. Let me just say I love my cousins. They are the only superhot and popular girls that I get to hang out with, and they also keep me laughing at the number of boys they turn down on a daily basis. However, they can be a bit clueless at times. They actually wanted me to tan with them; they seemed to have forgotten that I didn't really need a tan, because of my natural one. All three of us were getting out of the water, and I was ready to head to the ice-cream shop, and then Sarah said, "Oh, Fatima, where are you going? We were just about to lay out. I don't know about you, girl, but I prefer a natural tan." Katie agreed, she said, "I can't stand the tanning beds; they are so lame and you end up looking orange, but we'd rather go there than be all pasty white. That's why we love the summer. Oh, by the way, which one do you like best? I mean, you are already dark enough, but I would love to have your color in the summer. It would be awesome. I'm so pale!"

I laughed at them and told them I was good with my "natural tan" and would wait for them in the cool ice-cream shop while I munched down on a banana split. They simultaneously yelled at me as I turned to go, "Watch those calories, Tima." I laughed outright at them. They are notorious on-again-off-again dieters. My stomach was getting excited just thinking about the ice cream. I'd let their size-two bodies concentrate on calories while I concentrated on the taste of my ice cream.

I love my mom, but I think she really struggles at times trying to raise a black/white daughter. She just knows how to raise me as her mother raised her, as a privileged upper-middle-class white girl who never had to struggle a day in her life. For example, when my curly-like 'fro seemed to stress her out, she called up her one or two black girlfriends from college to ask them what products to buy or what beautician to see in order to make my hair smooth and straight.

I am not a Tiger Woods; I refuse to invent some crazy name to call myself in order to not identify with any of my true cultures. We see how that turned out for him in the end, right? Anyway, I guess I'm just plain tired and confused about the entire thing.

On my father's side of the family, they pretty much try to act like they are color-blind, but the comments they make about my mom from time to time can be hurtful. For example, "Why does every successful black man have to have a white woman on his arm? Lord, I thought our brother would have known better," my aunts discuss, clicking their tongues the entire time. "I mean, if your mama is black, then your woman should be black!" I usually clear my throat really loud, and they change the subject really quickly.

My grandmother on my father's side, however, does not care who is in the room. She completely believes in speaking her mind at all times. I call her Granny G, short for Greta Lee. She's a God-loving, home-cooking, outspoken diva and proud of it. One time when I was really young, I heard her tell my mom in a very casual way, "Look, girl, I don't know how you were raised, but my son was raised on home-cooked meals, so you need to take some of all that money he makes and get yourself some lessons, because picking up a menu every night is not being a good wife. And while I'm on the subject, my grandbaby need to know more than just your side of her family. She need to know all her people. My boy go off to college and bring home a white girl. Do, I look white? No. I am pecan tan, but don't get me wrong, girl, I love you, because I love God and all his creations, but you need to learn how to cook, and my grandbaby need to spend some time with her family so she'll know who she is." My mom in her ultra-positive way just agreed and smiled at all of this. Meanwhile the rest of the family was staring in shock.

My dad on the other hand was saying, "All right, Ma, that's enough. I didn't marry her for her cooking abilities. I married her because I love her, and she's a good woman. Remember, Ma, you told me a long time ago God honors marriages!"

Granny G responded, "Love is great, but what you going to do when your stomach is growling and your baby girl don't know her people?"

Eventually Daddy changed the subject because he knows that no one can argue with Granny G and win. I love Granny G, but her forthright attitude can be a bit overbearing and downright insulting at times.

Chapter 2

Say What?

*My People! Say it loud…I'm black/white and what?
Proud!
People stare hoping to understand how love can cross
The boundaries of cultures and yet span
eternity over races in the sand
How can we unite and equally combine
Must we all walk in this life blind?
I see nothing only the same tired old thing,
a lack of tolerance and the old historical struggle of pain
God, are we truly the same?*

—FATIMA

In today's society you really can't go many places without seeing one of "my kind." I know it's strange to think that we are now some type of new breed or something. It's all so stupid! I mean, at the end of the day people are people no matter the color. And the mixing of the races has been around for ages, but it just has become a bit more accepted by society. When I say a bit more accepted, I mean that you won't lose your life for dating outside of your race nowadays. I mean, don't get me wrong, we still get the glares and stares from people when we're shopping or at restaurants.

White men look at how hot my mom is and then they glare angrily when they see my dad come up behind her and place his arms lovingly around her waist. Black women look at my daddy like they could sop him up like a biscuit and gravy, and then they see me and my mom and roll their eyes and shake their heads. They try to do all of this without being seen, but me being the ever-observant person that I am, I see all and hear all. My parents, however, act as if they are oblivious and in their own little world of love.

The thing that I hate the most is that this stereotypical, ignorant, and prejudiced society we live in wants me to pick a side to be either black or white. At school, in my family, in public, wherever I go, I feel as if people are waiting to see how I'm going to act in order to determine how to classify me in their stereotypical categories. For example, if I'm at a restaurant, I try not to show how good my chicken really tastes, because I don't want the old chicken stereotype to pop up: "Black folks sho' love them some chicken, and don't forget the watermelon on the side." Or if I'm at the mall and the saleswoman is extra nice to me and looks down her nose at the other girl my age who just happens to be African American, I refuse to give that store my money. I think to myself, "This is my way of paying them back for their discrimination." However, later on I really wish I would have bought the cute skirt or shirt in the store, but I always end up standing my ground once I make a decision. I strongly support the right to boycott at all times; it must be in my blood.

Chapter 3

The Loner

I sit alone
The coldness of the stone step my only
knowledge that I'm still alive
My hands hold my head and my mind
holds back the tears I should cry
But, I refuse to, for there is comfort in my loneliness
I mean, who needs friends anyway?
Not me, I'd much rather just enjoy my own company
Only sometimes I feel sad,
And at times I can't understand…maybe God has a plan?
For me?

—FATIMA

In addition to being that mixed girl, I have one more thing to be grateful for in my life: I am a bit overweight. OK, if you want me to be totally honest, I am straight out and out FAT! Combine my shyness, my color complex, and my weight, and you have a great combination for middle-school success. That is why at school, I walked with my head down most of the time. I don't know why I just felt more comfortable that way. I hated to look into the eyes of some kid who would only reflect their disgust at my appearance. I was disgusted enough at myself. I knew I wasn't the prissy, pretty, prima-donna doll that most of my fellow female classmates were. I was a chunky, curly-and-wild-haired quiet girl with a bland face and hazel-green eyes. I kept to myself and walked mostly with my head down.

Unfortunately, walking with your head down can lead to upsetting some people. On a daily basis I heard, "Watch where you're going, fatso" or "Look up, blimp" or "Watch out for the fat girl." I actually started looking forward to the new and expressive comments from the idiots who yelled them out, just to see if I could come up with my own insulting reply, but instead of telling them the quirky comebacks I thought inside my head, I kept everything inside. Everything! When everyone started calling me Fatty Fatima (behind my back for the shy ones and straight in my face for the more bold soldiers), I kept that inside too. But what I really wanted to do was explode.

I was so thankful when we had only two months left of my eighth-grade school year. I counted down the days to summer, where I could once again spend my time reading and escaping the reality that was my life. I managed to make it to my first class without any trouble in the hallway. The middle-school section of the school was the smallest, so you didn't have to fight your way to get to class like we had done in elementary school. I mean, can you imagine a bunch of little people who were supposed to be walking in a single-file line, running wild while their young-and-clueless teachers tried to catch them and direct them to the correct class? Yeah, it was quite a sight.

Back then I actually had friends. If you can call the girls I hung out with friends. They were more interested in my lip gloss, candy, and sticker collection than they were in me. However, I was happy then. Middle school, on the other hand, was an entirely different story. Everyone paired off into cliques, and me? Well, let's just say I was the oddball out, so to speak.

My mom explained everything away like she always does. "Sweetie, maybe they just are expecting you to come up and talk to them."

I said, "No, Mom, I think that's not the case at all. When you walk up to a group of giggling girls, and they suddenly stop giggling and look at you as if you smell, I doubt they want to hang out with you."

My mom's reply? "Well, honey, I know you don't smell; you have excellent hygiene."

That's my mom; she always knows exactly what to say. After all, she is perfect. From her long, straight hair, almond-shaped eyes, and perfectly shaped body to her olive, blemish-free skin. She is the definition of perfection. She is God's great creation of 100 percent woman. I knew she was embarrassed by me, although she never said anything. I mean, if I looked like her and had a daughter like me, I would have been embarrassed too.

On one occasion we were at the mall shopping, and I was standing beside my mom in line, and this pretty, little brunette girl was standing in front of my mom, and the sales clerk actually told the girl, "Wow, you look just like your mom. The two of you could be models."

The girl looked at my mom and smiled and said, "She's not my mom, but she is really pretty though."

My mom, always the positive optimist that she is, looked at the sales clerk and pointed at me. She said, "This is my daughter, and she is probably prettier than me."

The sales clerk immediately took our money and told us to have a nice day.

I felt sorry for my parents; I mean, they were two very hot people! My father looked like he stepped from the cover of a GQ magazine. Yes, my dad is just as good-looking as my mom. He is six foot five with bright hazel-green eyes, a nice muscular build, and a perfectly featured face. They both make quite a couple. Unfortunately, they also made me, the blemish on their otherwise perfection.

Chapter 4

The New Me

So, I don't care what you think
Stare if you want, laugh, and grin showing all your teeth
Your opinion of me is as brief as a blink
I'm changing, you see
No longer hindered by you or them
I embrace my voice, I scream
And I rejoice, I'm new, and I'm me
So that makes me FREE!

—F<small>ATIMA</small>

Finding Fatima

It was Monday, the day I dread most in the week. As usual, I was the first one in my English class. I sat down and waited for everyone to pile into the room. I was usually the first one in all my classes. I hated to walk in with everyone already sitting down. I felt like they were all staring at me. I watched as Miss Snyde put our grammar warm-up on the SMART Board. I liked her; she was a good teacher. She always explained things well and provided positive responses to your papers instead of marking them all over with the dreaded red pen like Mr. Cutler did in History class. He loved to tell you you were going to get an F on a daily basis.

I considered myself a pretty good student; the work was easy. The truth is most of the time I was bored out of my mind. The only class I really looked forward to was Drama. I loved the theater because it was the only place where I couldn't care less what people thought about me. I would lose myself in my characters or improv, and forget that they were twenty more people in the room with me.

That Monday, Ashley and her groupies came into the room in their usual flair of perfume and preppiness. "Wow, Miss Snyde, your class stinks," Ashley said loudly so everyone could hear her.

Miss Snyde responded with her usual niceness. "Well, Ashley, get the spray and spray the room, honey," she replied.

Ashley, grinning from ear to ear, deliberately came near me and started spraying. I just looked at her and shook my head. I was starting to get sick and tired of her mess. I could just imagine myself punching her in her face until my fist grew tired. Instead, I raised my hand and asked Miss Snyde if I could use the bathroom. When I got to the bathroom, I sat down on the bench and tried to control my anger. I counted to ten, but it didn't work. I could feel the heat of my anger taking over my body. I knew that Ashley was just being a "mean girl," but I had had enough of being her target. My life was not one of those dumb movies where the outcast had to become the mean girl in order to fit in with the same idiots who mistreated her. I didn't want to fit in with a bunch of fake hateful little girls. I made my mind up that if they came at me, I would be ready! After three years of bullying from the same group of girls, I had reached my breaking point.

Chapter 5

Justifiable Injustice

*I am justifiable in my injustice
Because of my rage
After taking and taking it
I can no longer breathe. I need some release to help me cope
Contemplated walking away, but instead I decide to explode
I wonder will they leave me alone now
that they know I'm on fire?
Can you see the blaze from heaven?*

—*Fatima*

Finding Fatima

I was down to one more month left of school, and I could not have been happier. I checked each day off my calendar as if it were my worst enemy. Speaking of my worst enemies, me and Ashley had a showdown. I can't believe it, but for the first time I stood up to her, and she looked as if she was going to have a heart attack. We were at lunch and she and her groupies were walking by with their salads in hand, speaking in their usual high-pitch, frenzied voices. She stopped by me and placed a salad on the table and said with a touch of sarcasm, "This is my treat to you, for old times' sake when we used to be friends."

I looked at her; I looked at the salad. Back and forth my head went as I contemplated what my next move should be, and from that point on I knew that it was out of my control. The fate of the salad was determined. Before I could stop myself, I opened the salad container and threw the salad all over her, and before I could stop myself again, I picked up the dressing and plopped it in her hair and said, "Don't forget the dressing."

Then as I walked away from the group I added, "Thanks so much for the salad, Ashley, but it actually looks better on you. I know you are watching your calories, and by the way I think the dressing is low fat, just like you like it."

She stood there stupefied and outraged. When her shock was gone, she starting screaming all kinds of insults at me. "You fat black zebra! You round black Oreo, you stinking skunk! You will not get away with this!"

Her little minions grabbed napkins and exclaimed in shocked voices, "I can't believe she did that!"

"She is crazy!"

"What a psycho!"

Ashley marched out of the lunchroom with her entourage following her, trying to clean her up, but she angrily pushed them away. The entire lunchroom was watching me as I made my exit, and for the first time in my life I didn't care at all.

Of course no good deed goes unpunished. About thirty minutes into my third block class I was called out to see the dean. I walked with a spring in my step, because at that point I didn't care what they did to me.

Mr. Carter was not an attractive man; he was pale and rotund with thick glasses and a bald head. He tried to look stern when I entered the room, but instead he looked like a bald Santa Claus to me. I sat down and waited for the interrogation. It was the first time in my life I had been called in to see the "man," and surprisingly I wasn't scared at all. He just stared at me for what seemed like forever. After clearing his throat he started.

"Frankly, Fatima, I am really surprised at you. You are an honors student, and you have no record to speak of. What in the world would make you do something like this? Do you know that Ashley had to go home? Her entire outfit was ruined," he said.

I tried to hold my laughter in; her outfit was ruined from a salad? I mean, I can see her hair with the dressing and all, but she could have just brushed the lettuce off her clothes. I thought a moment before I spoke; I didn't know if I should be honest or lie and say how sorry I was. I decided to be honest.

"Mr. Carter, I am not sorry for what I did. The fact is if teachers and administration spent more time disciplining the students who deserved it, I wouldn't be in this predicament. From the time I was in sixth grade on up until now, Ashley and her little followers, and several other people in this school have tormented me on a daily basis just to amuse themselves. While teachers, administration, and counselors stood by and did nothing. Do you know what I'm sorry for? I'm sorry that teachers have selective hearing and only hear things when they are said about *them*. I've been called Fatty Fatima and zebra so many times I bet most of my teachers think they're my real names, but not once have they reprimanded the kids for calling me that. Instead they ignore the comments as if they were nothing. The fact is, Mr. Carter, I am tired of letting girls like Ashley think it's OK to treat people like they're nothing, and it's about time Ashley and the rest of her crew get what they deserve."

Mr. Carter looked like he was in a state of shock. I could tell it took him a while to gather his thoughts before he spoke. "Fatima, I'm sorry you feel that way, but you should have told an adult. They would have informed me, and you would not have gone through what you have for so long. Don't assume we know everything that goes on; we don't. We can't help you if we don't know there is a problem, now can we?" I thought he would stop to catch his breath, but he kept right on talking, breathing heavily. "It is the job of every teacher, administrator, and counselor in this school to make sure that you are looked after, and we don't take our jobs lightly. We have a zero-tolerance policy on bullying. That's our motto, and we stand by it strongly! I am upset that this has gone on this long and nothing has been done, but I can assure you that it will not be tolerated now that I know about it."

I was beyond angry by then; so I decided to really speak my mind. "Really, Mr. Carter, I don't know what world you live in, but I live on planet Earth. This group of girls hates everything about me! I'm sure they would stop bullying me if I just told all my teachers, spoke to the counselors and all the administrators about my problems. Then we could all go to the office holding hands and singing 'Cumbaya,' where we would then make up, hug one another, and become best friends for life. I've learned that it is my issue, and I have to deal with it the best way I know how. Throwing salad on her head was a lot nicer than punching her in the face. Anybody who has ever been in Ashley or her little Mini-Me's presence would know that they are hateful and spiteful people.

"I realize Ashley's family and their donations mean a great deal to this prestigious academy, but my parents pay good money for me to go here too, and I am sure they don't send me to school to be tormented. Thank God I'm not one of those kids who would go home and cut myself over their stupidity or one of those angry kids who would bring a bunch of guns to school and start blowing up the place. If you all were more concerned with the students as opposed to the money their parents pay to you and donate to your private funds, kids like me would be better off," I told him in a frustrated and hurried voice.

"Fatima, first of all I realize you are upset, but I will not tolerate disrespect, so mind your words. Secondly, when you say nothing, then nothing gets done. We are here to protect you, and look after you, but we can't read your minds. Teachers hear friends joking with one another every day, and when we call them on it, they say, 'Oh, we were just playing around.' How do they know the difference from a friendly joke or a more serious issue? You have to speak up and let us know what is going on. I don't care how many checks or donations are made out, you are just as important as any other child, and I will not have you tormented. Our academy is for rigorous learning, not this…this bullying you speak of to me. I will handle this today, and parents will be informed, and it will not continue. You have my word," Mr. Carter said.

I stared at his red, agitated face, and I knew that he meant everything he said. I did not want my parents involved. My mother had been threatening me with counseling for years, and I knew that this would be the tool she needed to make me go. "Please, Mr. Carter, I don't want my parents to know about this. I'm sure things will just blow over and everything will go back to normal. I'll try not to let it happen again," I meekly told him.

He gave me a weird look and then said, "I'm sorry, Fatima, I have no choice, and it has gone on long enough. I will be contacting parents, and the next time it happens I will give disciplinary action against the perpetrator. At this time, based on what you've told me and since this is your first offense, I will let you go with a warning. Now, go back to class, and if you have any problem with any other student just ask to speak to me directly from now on. Take care, and I hope to hear good things from here on out from or about you."

I raced from the stuffy office and prayed that he would forget about calling parents, but I knew that he wouldn't. Instead of going back to my class I decided to spend the rest of the day in the library…I knew if I went back to class it would be straight drama. The library was a welcome escape for me. Books always seemed to be kinder than real people. I skipped the rest of my classes for the rest of the day and stayed in the library reading until I heard the dismissal bell. The good thing about my library was that it was huge, and you could hide out in the cubbies without being found for hours. I knew that no one would come looking for me because they would all assume I was in big trouble for messing with the untouchable Ashley Leigh Lewis.

As soon as the bell rang, I raced outside and got in my mom's car. I was not in the mood for her hyper chitchat, so I immediately put my earbuds in my ears. I turned the music on my iPhone up on full blast, and I laid the seat back to relax. I was so thankful it was Friday, and I had two days to reflect on the new me and the changes I wanted to make…I also knew that I would have to talk to my parents about what happened, and I was not looking forward to that before Bald Santa—I mean Mr. Carter—made that dreaded phone call to them.

Surprisingly, on the ride home from school, my mom didn't ask me twenty questions like she usually did each day. Instead she was painfully quiet. I was used to her forcing me to take my earbuds off and turn my iPhone off so I could listen to her drill me about my day. She just kept looking over at me with a worried look on her face. When we got home, I saw that my dad was home early from work, and I knew an intervention and a long lecture was headed my way.

Mom parked, and she got out of the car. I sat there hoping that she would forget that she had a daughter, but of course she didn't. "Come on, Fatima, your dad is waiting for us," she said.

I reluctantly left the comfort of the car and headed in the house, where my dad, still dressed in his suit from work, stood pacing the foyer of the house. When we walked in, he stopped his pacing and looked up with real concern in his handsome face. "Baby, you OK?" he asked. I just nodded my head. My dad was the one person on earth who could make me cry with just a few words, and I felt my eyes watering. I felt like he really understood me most of the time.

Dad told me to follow him and Mom into the family room; I guess the superglitzy living room was too pretty for the ugliness of our conversation. Mom started talking first, which was surprising; I thought she was going to give this episode of parenting over to Dad. "Sweetie, Mr. Carter called us today, and he had some very disturbing news to share. First of all, I want you to know that if you are ever going through anything, you can come to us at any time. You shouldn't hold it in; it's not healthy. We are here for you, to help you with everything you go through, but we can't help you if we don't know you need it," my mom said with tears in her eyes. That's my mom, the sensitive one. If an animal was hurt along the side of the road, she's the one who would pick it up and take it to the vet, and pay to have it taken care of no matter the cost. I guess she couldn't understand how her daughter could be so unpopular, when she was the most popular and prettiest girl in her school.

I looked at her and shook my head. "Mom, don't cry. It's not that deep. Ashley deserved what she got, and it was just a salad; I don't know why everyone is acting like I punched her in the face or something, I mean, geesh, maybe I should have since it turned out to be a big deal anyway. I've decided that from now on I am not going to let her and her little groupies lower my self-esteem with their hateful intentions," I told her with anger in my voice.

My dad, who had stopped pacing, and was letting my mom take the lead, decided it was time for him to enter the conversation. "Tima, look, honey, when you give in to your anger and stoop to the level of people like that, you are just lowering yourself to their standards, which, from what I understand, are not that high. We are raising you to be strong and independent, but we also want you to know that you do not have to tolerate abuse from anyone. I don't care if it is verbal, physical, or anything else. We don't pay thousands of dollars for you to go to school and be tormented by a group of girls who think they are the best thing since sliced bread. I will not tolerate it," my father roared.

I had seen my father upset like this only one time, and that was when I played softball and the girl had purposefully thrown the ball as hard as she could at my head. He stormed on the field and made the coaches stop the game and take the pitcher out of the game. He demanded she apologize and be benched for the season. Everybody on the field that day knew my father meant business, and no one dared say a word to him. My mom had run to take care of me while my dad proceeded to let slip some words that I didn't even know he had in his vocabulary.

Finding Fatima

It felt like their lecture lasted two hours, but I guess it only lasted a few minutes. They made it clear that I was to let them know if I had a problem, and to let an adult know before taking matters into my own hands. My mom even mentioned a dreaded counselor session, which I shook my head at before the words left her lips. I did not need someone trying to get inside my head. I had enough going on inside there, and I did not need anyone intruding on that space.

My dad sternly looked at me after the lecture was over, and said with a half smile, "Miss Ashley better be glad you didn't give her that powerful right hook I taught you to use to defend yourself, or her face would have been messed up along with her hair."

I smiled at him and shook my head. My dad had a way of lightening up a situation. I sure had thought about using my fist, though, but I knew that would have been an automatic suspension even if I had a clean record. My mom and dad both hugged me and told me how much they loved me, as if I didn't know that already, and I escaped to my room for the night.

Chapter 6

Love

Love,
Read about, dreamed about, thought about It
But I've never really felt its presence
Until he entered my life
Strong, powerful beauty in a man
If only I stood a chance
Could I have a shot at real romance?
Didn't you make me to fall in love?

—FATIMA

Finding Fatima

It was as if I gained my freedom that day I stood up to Ashley in the cafeteria. It seemed that every day after that I gradually changed more and more. Some would say my change was not positive. Well, actually only my mom would say that. I couldn't really care less, though. Instead of keeping everything I wanted to say bottled up inside, I started saying what I felt, doing what I felt, and expressing myself...without fear of what anyone thought about me.

It was funny, but the hypocritical kids at my school who had refused to speak to me before started saying hi, as if I was the president's daughter. It seemed like every day someone who had never spoken to me before was waving at me or calling my name as I walked in the hall or in class. I even had people volunteering to be my partner in PE and Chemistry Lab.

However, the best part of it all was that I got to finally snub those popular kids who had treated me so badly. On top of that I found some true kindred spirits to hang out with. They were not the most popular girls. We were a bunch of misfits, but ironically enough we made sense together. They also had been tormented by Ashley and her minions, and they congratulated me as if I had won an Oscar for standing up to her and keeping my ground. In a short amount of time I grew to love the girls, and I was sad that we became friends so late in the year. But what made me really happy about knowing them was that they were genuine people and really cared about me.

My group of girls was Janet, a pretty Asian girl with punk-rock pink hair and thick eyeglasses—she said contacts irritated her allergies too bad; Debbie, a short black girl with braids and a quirky, dry sense of humor—who was bound to be the class valedictorian because she was a brainiac and proud of it; Regina, an almost-six-foot blond Caucasian ballerina with perfect posture and a slight lisp; and Jackie, a mixed girl with an identity issue, just like me. We were all a perfect match. This was my new group of friends. We knew we didn't fit in, but we didn't care. We even started calling ourselves the Misfits, and we were proud! I still maintained my grades of course; I refused to let my grades suffer just because I was experimenting with a new-and-improved "I don't care" attitude.

Anyway, my mom was in a constant state of perplexity with the way I spoke my mind around the house. "Fatima, I don't know what has happened to you. Where is my sweet little girl? Your mouth has become so grown and sassy I'm thinking about sending you to Granny G this summer instead of fitness camp; she'll set you straight in a minute."

Of course my reply was, "Mother, number one, Granny G loves me, and she's never reprimanded me in my life—except for the time I ate the cake she had made for church—and number two, it's 'fat camp,' not 'fitness camp.' Now do you want to go to Dairy Queen? Because I could really go for a strawberry milk shake."

My mom shook her head, and I went upstairs to my room, because in the next instant that would be her punishment for what she called my "newfound sassiness." I thought back to all the times when I would just go along with whatever my mom wanted me to do, thinking that I was being a good child. In reality I was just being who she wanted me to be, not myself. All the times she would make me squeeze into Hollister, stuff myself into American Eagle, Abercrombie and Fitch, and Banana Republic clothing, because that's what all her friends' daughters were wearing. Also, the numerous visits to the salon to straighten out my natural curly or, as she would say, "kinky" hair. I really love my mom, don't get me wrong, but it's really difficult living your life trying to be the perfect child to the perfect woman. Since my situation at school she had been once again threatening to send me to a counselor, and I told her to take it easy; I could only handle one punishment at a time. I already was trying to talk myself out of fat camp.

Thursday was the second best day of the school week. I walked in my Algebra class just in time to see that a new student was standing next to Miss Lane; he was the most attractive male specimen I had ever seen in my life. I had things for Spanish, African American, and Caucasian Nordic-type guys. Let's just say this guy was a combination that even my dreams could not put together. He was tall, with a medium build; I could see his fit muscles through his Polo shirt. He had tan skin, light-green eyes, perfect teeth, dimples, and a strong jawline. He looked like a Greek warrior, and I would love to be his captured damsel. OK, so he was from Colombia and his name was Jorge, but a girl could use her romance-novel dreams, right?

Anyway, I could see the other girls in the class staring him down, and I felt the sting of jealousy hit me. I mean, honestly he probably would not give me a second glance with my pudgy body, but they, with their skinny bones poking out, long hair, and big eyes and smile would probably be able to snap him up in a heartbeat. Of course he sat next to Ashley, and that made my heart sink even lower. Although she had a steady boyfriend who worshiped her at every turn, she still had the nerve to give Jorge a coy smile and wink. I wanted to really slap her this time, but instead I played it cool. I would hide my secret crush, and one day I would get the opportunity to let Jorge know that he and I were a perfect match.

Not only was he extra fine, but he also seemed to be pretty smart. He actually volunteered to go to the board several times, and he knew the answers to problems I didn't even know. Some of the knucklehead boys in the class were coughing and saying under their breaths, "Try hard."

Jorge responded, "Well, you don't have to try when it's an easy sixth-grade problem. Maybe you all should try harder!" I knew then that I was in love. His arrogance was just enough to make me pledge myself to him for life, even if he didn't know I existed.

I was so excited to go to Granny G's for the weekend that I didn't realize my parents were dropping me off to go on one of their weekend getaways; I couldn't have cared less, though, because I was on my way to some good eating and some live entertainment. Something interesting was always happening at her house or at her church. My stomach was quivering in anticipation for the delicious home-cooked meal Granny G would prepare. (My mom had learned how to cook. The problem was it was all healthy, flavorless crap!) I figured that if my parents were going to send me to fat camp and make me lose weight, I might as well give them their money's worth for the super-expensive program they were going to have to pay for.

I packed my bags in record time, and I was waiting for my parents in the Hummer before they could make it out the front door of the house.

The trip was short and sweet, just like I liked. I didn't even give my parents time to say good-bye before I was running inside Granny G's. "Have fun!" I yelled behind me as I banged on Granny's front door.

My uncle Bruce opened the front door. He was living with Granny G. He had gone through a really tough divorce, and he still hadn't recovered from it. "Hey, baby girl," he said, picking me up into a huge bear hug. I could hardly breathe. Then he landed the sloppiest wet kiss on my cheek. He had to know that I was getting too old for hugs.

I hugged him back, and tried to breathe at the same time, he was definitely notorious for his bear hugs. "Hey, Uncle Bruce, how are you?" I asked.

"I'm good, baby. My construction business is finally getting on its feet again, and I am about to close on a new condo. It's not as fancy as the house I used to have, but things are finally starting to look up for me."

"Good," I said. "I'm so glad to hear that," I told him. I really was. I had missed my uncle. He had been so fun and full of life when I was younger, and after his divorce he had turned into a depressed, boring coach potato. His wife had decided to leave him and file for divorce after his construction business went bankrupt. I overheard my aunts say that she had cheated on my uncle, and that she had a new man before they even separated. Marriage was no joke, it made me wonder if I would ever tie the knot.

I could smell something delicious coming from the kitchen, so I cut my conversation with one of my favorite uncles short while I made my way to the kitchen to see what Granny G was preparing. He didn't seem to mind, because he confided in me that he had a new girlfriend and that they had made plans to go on a hot date that night. I smiled and shook my head. I guess even old people need love.

"Hey, baby. I didn't know you were here yet. Give me a hug," Granny G said. Granny G always smelled like peaches 'n' cream, or whatever food she was busy preparing. I looked around and discovered that Granny G was making some of my favorite things to eat: fried pork chops, baked apples, rice and gravy, mac 'n' cheese. It felt like Sunday dinner, but it was only Friday afternoon.

"Baby, after we eat," she said, "we gonna watch some movies and talk while we munch down on this chocolate bread pudding and ice cream." Granny G's cooking was famous; she was a widow who raised six children off of being one of the best soul-food cooks in Richmond, VA. When the restaurant she had worked at for twenty years was about to close, she got a loan from a bank based on her name alone, bought the place, and made the restaurant an even greater success overnight. She paid the bank off and was able to send all six of her children to college. My daddy may have had a few struggles growing up, but my Granny G made sure that they all valued their education and went on to be strong men and women, both financially and spiritually. My uncle Mike and aunt Shirley took over the restaurant after she retired, and now there are three Southern Fried Goodness restaurants throughout Virginia.

After eating dinner and dessert I rolled myself to the couch, where I stayed for the rest of the night. Instead of watching a movie like we were supposed to do, Granny G and I both fell fast asleep, me stretched out on her sofa, and her reclined back in her favorite La-Z-Boy.

The next morning I awoke with one of my granny G's quilts thrown over me, and I could smell cheese biscuits and bacon. I thought my stomach should still be full from last night's over indulgence, but it managed to let out a growl at the smell of the delicious aromas coming from the kitchen. "Rise and shine, sleepyhead," Granny G said. "You were sleeping so peacefully on the couch, I just couldn't bring myself to wake you up. The church is having a bake sale today to raise money for the Cancer Walkathon. I baked a bunch of stuff yesterday before you came and took it out to the church. This morning I'm going to focus on getting the last of my pies, brownies, and puddings. You are welcome to stay here or you can come on out to the church and help me," Granny G said.

I gave it some thought. I liked Granny G's church; it was always something interesting happening there. I could watch TV anytime, so I decided to go shower and get dressed. It was hot, so I chose to wear a navy-blue, sleeveless cotton dress I had gotten from Gap, with some dressy flip-flops.

We loaded everything into the car and headed to St. Luke Missionary Baptist Church.

When we got there, the huge church was packed with people outside set up with different tables of sweets. This was not your ordinary grocery-store bake sale; this was a huge event. There were people and food everywhere. Granny G led me to her table and went inside the church to get the rest of her baked goods while I set her table up. I was already sweating by the time I put the table cloth on the table, priced all the items that were outside, and waited for Granny G to return. She came out of the church about twenty minutes later with slices of individually wrapped cake, cookies, and brownies.

"I know, baby," she said, "this is the biggest bake sale you have ever seen, huh? Well, girl, in about thirty minutes all this food is going to disappear. People come from all over to get my sweets, and by the time they get here, I'm usually sold out."

Sure enough, once the bake sale officially started, our line was the longest in the church's park-and-recreation area. Everybody knew my granny G and everybody wanted her sweets. While I was sitting there trying to keep up with the purchases, wipe the sweat from my forehead, and give back the correct change to people, you would not believe who showed up. Yes, Jorge. Mr. Fine Colombian himself came up asking for some bread pudding. I tried to get my granny G's attention—I did not want to wait on him—but she was busy having a conversation with Mrs. Bertie, a neighbor who lived across the street, about her cataract surgery. It was do or die. I had to speak to my dream boy.

I asked him what type of bread pudding he wanted, and he said, "I don't know; you can surprise me," because he had never had it before, but everyone else at the sale was walking around talking about how delicious it was, so he wanted to try it for himself. I tried not to let his hot accent bother me, but I was shaking as I handed him the chocolate bread pudding. I told him that it was my favorite and that most people had bought it. He looked at me with a big smile on his face and handed me a five-dollar bill, saying, "You can keep the change." And then he said the craziest thing. "I'll see you at school on Monday, Fatima."

I was dumbfounded. Not only did he recognize me, but he knew my name as well. Granny G looked at me and said, "Baby, you better close your mouth before you catch a fly in there. I'm sweating from head to toe. I think we've made enough money for one day, and we only have a few pieces of bread pudding and two pies left anyway, Fatima. Let's get out of this hot sun."

Chapter 7

Say My Name

What's in a name?
Me? Yes, indeed you are the one I need
Oh dear, I am thrilled
These emotions got me reeling…and the sound
of my name on those lips is very appealing
But then I wake up and I realize
You called me in dream
I decide to go back to sleep,
Hoping to find you when I close my eyes

—Fatima

Finding Fatima

The weekend with Granny G turned out to be one of the most important weekends of my life. I could not stop thinking about Jorge. On Monday, I took extra care with my hair. I used a new conditioner my mom had bought for me that loosened my curls and made them less frizzy; I wore one of my best outfits, a black-and-white stripped maxi dress with red wedge shoes; and I even applied some makeup to my face,—eye shadow, lip gloss, and a little eyeliner to enhance the green in my eyes.

That morning, my dad, who always complimented me on how pretty I was anyway, did a double take at the breakfast table. "Fa-teeeem-uh." He whistled. "You are looking just lovely this morning. Get over here and give your old daddy some sugar, and you better not be dressing like that for a little boy. I might have to come to that school and beat up on somebody," Dad said in his most manly voice.

In class I kept hoping to get Jorge's attention, but he didn't even look my way. At the end of class, I tried to leave out as fast as I could because I thought I was about to have a breakdown. I realized that Jorge knowing my name was not a big deal; I was just some fat girl to him that knew a great deal about bread pudding—nothing more, nothing less. I walked out of the room with my head down for the first time in weeks.

I was so focused on my sadness that, at first, I did not hear my name being called. "Fatima, Fatima." When I realized what I was hearing, I turned around and stared into the eyes of Jorge. "I just wanted to tell you that the bread pudding was one of the best things I have ever eaten in my life," he said. "Your grandmother should open a restaurant."

I was speechless. I mean, what was I supposed to say to him? Should I confess my undying love for him and promise to feed him bread pudding every day as long as he stayed with me? I decided that would probably scare him away, so I just smiled at him and let him know that my grandmother actually owned three restaurants. He asked me for the name of them, and told me he was going to probably be eating dinner at her restaurants every night for the rest of his life, with a big smile. He patted me on the shoulder and said, "Well, I'll see you around."

After my daze left me, I saw some girls standing around glaring at me as if I had just stolen their boyfriend. I had never been the envy of anyone, but I guess there's a first time for everything.

Unfortunately, a few weeks later, my "relationship" with Jorge was not going well at all. Other than a wave from time to time or a "Hey, Fatima," he hardly knew I existed. He also seemed to have settled on a girl at our school. I hated to admit it, but he actually chose one of the nice ones. She was extremely gorgeous, but extra friendly and nice to everyone. Her name was Gloria, and she was from the Dominican Republic. She was tall, heavy up top with a Coca-Cola-bottle shape, and large hazel eyes, dimples, and full lips. Whenever I saw them together, I had to turn my head or pretend to be busy; the pain of sharing him was more than I could bear.

A few more weeks went by, and I saw how in love Gloria and Jorge seemed to be, and I decided it was time for me to let him go. It took me some time to get over my first crush, but eventually I was able to move on and focus on my newfound friendships with my lunchroom crew, and the fact that high school was looming over me in the not-so-distant future.

Chapter 8

My Girls

Chitchat, chatty, chatter,
Laughter and giggling lip gloss splatters
On my Levi jeans, finally got a group
that I can call my fellow queens
Please believe we reign supreme
Well, at least in the land of misfits we do,
I for the first time actually feel like part of a group
My girls, each unique and set apart
Wonderful creatures painted by his hand
We encircle our arms and embrace, we are glued together
By silly bands and our flowing scarves tied to our outcast states

—FATIMA

J. W. Hoffman

The school days were going by so fast I could hardly mark them off my calendar. I was not ready for summer. My mom had threatened me with fat camp or, as she called it "fitness camp," all year, and I absolutely did not want to go. I tried to get my dad to sympathize with me, but he seemed to be really excited about the camp experience with the lake, hiking, canoeing etc., etc., I knew my mom had brainwashed him before I could get to him. It was too late. My fate was decided, I was going to have to go.

My group of girlfriends branched out. We decided to move our friendship further than the lunchroom. We grew very close and started hanging out not only in school but also outside of school as well. I had almost forgotten what it felt like to be a part of a group and have real people to talk to and hang out with. My mom was over the moon about my newfound group of girlfriends. However, she didn't like the fact that we lovingly always referred to ourselves as the 'Misfits.' She suggested we call ourselves something more positive, but we laughed and told her we loved our name. The cool thing about my mom is that she would take us just about anywhere we asked to go. We hung at the mall, the movies, and the skating rink, and we went to all the cool school functions together. We decided to go out with a bang and represent big time at the eighth grade dance. Instead of wearing prom dresses like all the other girls would be wearing at the dance, we all went shopping and bought color-coordinated outfits to match. We each wore crazy fluorescent makeup to match our dark-blue skinny jeans and our bright-fluorescent off-the-shoulder shirts, with white tank tops under them. Each one of us had a different word embossed on our T-shirts in white, glittery letters. Mine said "SASSY." I thought I should put my mom's favorite new name for me to good use. We had the shirts made especially for the dance.

We were doing an ode to the eighties, and each one of use made our hair ridiculously big. We used over four cans of hair spray among us. I didn't need much spray; my crazy hair did its own thing anyway. We all wore matching white high-top Nikes we'd custom designed online, with the matching fluorescent color of our shirts in the Nike sign. You could not tell us we didn't look like teen models. We knew we were the stuff. I tried not to let the fact that I was the only girl in the group with skinny jeans that were plus size affect me too much. The girls assured me that I looked hot!

We arrived at the dance about an hour after it had started, and all eyes were on us. Some people clapped at our chosen dress code, and other people just laughed at us. We knew we would get attention, but negative or positive, we had decided we didn't care. We immediately found a neat spot to hang out on the dance floor. We started dancing as soon as our feet hit the floor, and not to brag, but I have crazy moves on the dance floor. My dad told me I took after my aunts; they were all dancing queens. The girls and I started our own soul train line, and then soon we had more than thirty kids gathered around, kicking their legs in the air, robot dancing, and spinning around like they were on fire.

We had gotten the party started, and it was in full form when you know who and her crew came in wearing these form-fitting, strapless spandex dresses that left little to the imagination. I thought the school had a dress code, but I guess not where little Miss Rich Girl is concerned. I refused to even acknowledge their presence. All the guys of course started salivating.

Anyway, I was dancing and moving around the floor with Debbie, who just happened to be my closest friend out of the group, and we were having a ball when she nudged me to look at this guy. "Girl, he is so fine, you really should go up to him and ask him to dance with you."

His name was Jack, and he was very popular and very cute. I looked at her as if she had sprouted horns and replied, "If you think he is so hot, why don't you ask him to dance?"

"Girl, that is not my style. He looks more like your type. He favors your man Jorge a little."

"First of all, Deb darling, you know I am still getting over that terrible heartbreak, and furthermore, he looks like he is way too into himself for me." Deep down, I wished I was brave enough to go over and talk to him. I knew that I did not stand a chance with him, especially since I was a chunky monkey and he was a hottie that every girl in the entire school probably loved. Deb walked away to go grab something to drink, and I just stood there standing like a lost puppy.

I stared in his direction and watched as Ashley and her crew circled him like an animal circling its prey. Ashley caught me looking over at Jack, gave me an ugly sneer, and started rubbing all over his chest. I turned my head in frustration. That was definitely a sight I did not want to see. When I went to find my girls, they were each on the floor with a guy dancing, and once again I felt like the odd girl out.

I plopped against the wall. I guess I was going to be the largest wallflower at the dance, because my prospects were slim. Nigel Winters was about two feet tall, and he had taken a book to the dance so he could read. How he managed to do that in a dimly lit room, I can't even imagine. Derek Case was too busy eating from the buffet of sweets to even consider a dance. Jorge Santana, the love of my life, was hugged up with Gloria. I couldn't stand to look at the perfect couple.

Finally, I couldn't take it anymore. I looked over again to Jack. He was standing by himself looking totally bored. I don't know what came over me, but I started walking in his direction. It was like my feet had a will of their own. I stepped up to him and asked in a loud voice so that he could hear me over the music, "Do you want to dance?"

He kind of stared at me for a while, and then he smiled at me. My heart skipped a beat. His smile was like sunshine in the morning. And then, it happened, he spoke to me.

"Look, you have a cute face and all, but I'm just not into fat girls. I like my girls slim and trim. I saw you over there looking at me, and I was hoping you wouldn't come over because I'm the type of guy who believes in being honest with a lady, even a big girl like yourself; I mean, I don't want to hurt your feelings or anything, but you're just not my type. I mean you have to know that you're fat right? But on a good note, I don't like any of the girls at this wack dance, so that should make you feel better. I'm into older, more experienced chicks, not little girls playing dress up," he said in a demeaning voice.

I was humiliated beyond belief. I didn't know if I should speak or just turn and run away in shame. I wanted to do the latter. Tears were welling in my eyes trying to escape, but I refused to let them fall. Instead, I turned around and started to leave, but something would not let me go. I turned back around, looked him straight in his handsome face, and decided to give him a piece of my mind.

"You know, you're right. I am a 'fat girl,' and I may not be your type, but the moment you opened your 'handsome,' vile mouth, I figured out you're not my type either. You are just a want-to-be-grown-up little boy with a nasty mouth full of arrogance, and I know why you are named Jack, because you're an Ass!" I screamed at him.

I turned away before he could respond. I ran over to my girls, who were finally free of the guys who had been practically hanging off of them, and we started dancing in a circle on the dance floor, doing our own thing. I refused to even glance in Jack's direction to see if he was seething with rage or still ever-so-coolly leaning against the wall.

That night when I finally got home from the dance, I threw myself on my bed and let the tears I'd felt at the dance flow free. I felt an array of emotions inside. I knew something had to change, but I didn't know how it was going to happen. I wanted people to see me—the real me, not the fat girl on the outside. But I also could not stand the superficial crap that people were into. It made me sick on my stomach to think that people only saw beauty and nothing else. I guess that's why I sort of liked having my outside layer; it was a defense mechanism against fake people. If people in the world spent more time perfecting the goodness they had on the inside instead of looking at the beauty on the outside of a person this world would be a better place. Yes, so what, I liked to eat, big deal. At least, I wasn't a hateful stuck-up butthole!

Chapter 9

Celebration

Shout, scream, dance it out!
Why do we celebrate?
Can I cram one day into a lifetime of years?
I walk across the stage and feel the eyes on my back
My crossing one stage for the next
Supposed to grow up, but inside I'm still a kid,
I wonder when my outside will truly be the inside
person who represents how I truly feel
What is my identity?

—F*atima*

Finding Fatima

So the day had finally arrived: my middle-school graduation. I was both happy and a little scared. I mean, I hated middle school, but high school could be even worse. I guess I should have been optimistic—one chapter closed, and another one opening up for me.

"Honey, you're going to be late. Hurry up. You don't want to miss your eighth-grade graduation, do you?" my mom called up to me. I looked again at my reflection with a grimace. The dress my mom had picked out was really pretty; it would look really good on someone else, not me. I was happy to cover it up with the blue cap and gown.

I headed down the stairs and tried to run from my father, who was excitedly holding a video camera. "I can't believe it. My baby is going to high school. My baby is graduating," he said with this big, goofy grin on his handsome face. My father refused to put the video camera away, even after I bribed him with a hug and a kiss. He took my hug and stole two extra kisses and still snuck and hid the camera behind his back.

We headed to the ceremony and arrived just in time for me to find my place in line outside. I had to shoo my parents into the auditorium. They wanted to videotape every single second of my "graduation experience." I wanted to run away from them in embarrassment. I finally managed to make them go inside, and I stepped into line just in time to start the graduation march.

The ceremony, like all ceremonies, was the most boring thing to sit through. The only highlight was the fact that a group of guys had snuck bubbles under their gowns and started blowing them in the face of the dean as he tried to hand out the certificates. Eventually the culprits were reprimanded, and the show went on uninterrupted until the end.

My parents had made reservations at Ruth Chris, and they had invited all the family. My aunt Jennifer and uncle Jackson on my mom's side, and my three aunts, Paula, Janet, and Shirley, and two uncles, Bruce and Mike, on my dad's side. They all took their husbands and wives and children along as well. My grandparents on my mom's side were there, and so was Granny G and her boyfriend Mr. Jeffrey, which was guaranteed to be a hit, because they all have a love/hate relationship. My godparents, who

I love, were in attendance as well. I call them my "hippy dippy" parents. Teddy and Becka are hilarious. I love weekends at their house because they always have some new cause they are fighting for or some experiment to try out, and yet they still eat junk food!

My family is very large, and lucky me, I was going to be in the spotlight. I didn't realize an eighth-grade graduation was such a big deal. They all acted as if I had just finished college. I knew my mom was behind it all; she seized any moment to throw a party and send out invitations. And I'm sure no one wanted to miss a free meal at a restaurant that charged almost fifty bucks a plate.

We got to the restaurant on time, despite my mom's insistence that she had to change out of her gorgeous dress in order to put on an even more gorgeous dress that fit her like a second skin and matched her hazel-green eyes. I shed my cap and gown and ran in to the restaurant to see my family. They were already seated and waiting for us.

My grandfather and Mr. Jeffrey were already in a heated debate about the state of the government, one democrat against one republican. They were in the age-old debate of who's right and who's wrong. My grandpa, who was quite the comedian, said, "Look, what I'm saying is the President should have really taken a look at revamping his campaign slogan from 'Yes, we can!' to 'No, I didn't.' This economy is horrible. I mean, the gas prices are so high people can't even afford to drive to work, and the unemployment line is so long people have to wait outside for days just to get inside the building to sit down in the waiting room. Don't get me started on the healthcare issues we have. But it doesn't matter now though because the candidates we have to choose from are just as pitiful; I'm going to have to pack my bags and move to Canada."

In retaliation, the democrat, Mr. Jeffrey said, "Man, you don't know nothing about politics. The President had to come into office with a huge broom just to sweep up the limbs and leaves your boy left behind. He left massive destruction when he left the office and a recession-like deficit in his wake, but I know he's just a good ol' boy with the right lineage and blue

Finding Fatima

blood, so the people voted him in without checking to see if he actually graduated from college, and your new candidate is literary an orange hot mess!"

My dad, always the peacemaker, broke up the discussion as soon as it caught his ears. "Look now, young men, today is my baby girl's day. No politics at the table."

Nana, my mom's mom, asked me, "Honey, when are you leaving for fitness camp?"

I said, "Nana, you mean 'fat camp,' and I guess my dear parents are shipping me out tomorrow, or that's when I'm scheduled to leave."

Nana sighed. "We had planned to take you with us on the cruise before you had to leave. You mean you have to go so fast? You just got out of school," Nana said.

I smiled inside as my Nana gave my mom a disapproving stare across the table. My mom couldn't stand it; she was forced to reply, "Mom, I know you wanted her to go with you, but there is always next summer. Fatima's health is more important than a cruise to the Bahamas, don't you think?" Mom asked.

"I'm not saying it isn't, dear, but we made these plans earlier in the year, and you know we always plan a nice getaway with Fatima each year, so that should have been considered when you made this fitness camp decision as well, shouldn't it have been, Jessica Diana Richards?" my Nana said.

I couldn't hold my laugh in any longer. When my Nana used my mom's full name, she was in big trouble. Luckily for her, my aunt Jennifer stepped in to rescue her. "OK mom, Jess gets it. We know you take the kids on a vacation each year. Just let it go so we can eat in peace, please?" my aunt said.

I'm not sure if my Granny G had her hearing aid in because it appeared she missed the entire argument. She said, "Baby, don't you listen to them. You just have a little baby fat. You'll grow out of it. You're still a pretty girl." I buried my head in the menu. I could tell that this was going to be a long dinner, and I was not looking forward to it at all.

About two hours later we left the restaurant and headed home. I was crazy tired, but I wanted to see my friends before my parents shipped me off to fat camp. So I talked my dad into stopping me by each of my girlfriends' houses to say good-bye. My mom wanted to go straight home to get out of her tight dress, but my dad won her over with one of his killer smiles, and she just started grinning like a little girl and agreed to go along for the ride.

We stopped at Debbie's house first; her driveway was full of cars as if some big party was in full swing. I knocked on the door, and Debbie's hot brother Brandon answered the door. "Oh, hi, come on in. I'll go get Deb. Sorry you had to miss the graduation party. The entire family is here as you can see; we roll deep."

I smiled at him and waited patiently in the foyer for Deb. She ran up to me, smiling and throwing her arms around me in a huge hug. "Girl, what's up? Graduation was so wack, wasn't it? Anyway girl, we are straight partying it up over here. My parents even let me taste a little sip of wine for the first time. You want me to get you some?" Deb asked. I shook my head no, and she continued her non-stop talking about graduation and the fun time she was having at her party.

In between her chatter, I was able to briefly tell her about fat camp and all the stupid rules. Deb responded, "What, fat camp? That sucks; I thought you were going to talk them out of it. Didn't work, did it? That really sucks. I hate that for you. Well, girl, I love you, and I am going to miss you so much. No phone calls, that really sucks. Sounds more like prison then a camp. Smooches and hugs, forever friends, love ya. Bye, boo."

You're probably wandering why I didn't respond much. Well, you should know that Deb has this problem with having a real conversation. Most of the time I listen and she talks. Anyway, one down, and three to go.

I got to Regina's house, and it looked empty at first, but then I saw Regina and her parents and little sister walking from around the huge, green, and lush backyard. Regina started waving wildly at me and ran up as if she was in a race. "Girl, save me," she breathed at me. "My parents are lecturing me about my future, my life, and college, and I haven't even

Finding Fatima

started high school yet. I want to enjoy my summer, not get worried to death. After an elegant dinner at Cheap Buffet, my parents wanted to go for a family walk to discuss things. It's been more like a family disaster. I'm tired of walking and tired of listening to them. Save me!" she said.

Things to note about Regina: First of all, her parents are both college professors and published authors. Although very successful and financially secure, they are supercheap, nature people, and ultra-overbearing about life. I looked at Regina in pity, and said, "Sweetie, I would love to take you away from it all, but I'm headed off to fat camp tomorrow, so my fate is just as depressing as yours. Maybe you can escape to one of the other girls' houses for the summer," I told her.

Regina shook her head. "No such luck. Thanks to my early birthday, a worker's permit, and my parents, I'll be completing an internship at the library at the university, so I start work tomorrow."

I almost choked on my tongue. "An internship, like a real job? We just left middle school. Are they serious?" I asked.

"Yes, they are serious, and the small, one-time stipend it pays for all of my hard work will go straight to the bank. Every single dime I get for anything has to be put away for my college education. I need serious help. You have to save me from my parents," Regina screamed.

I laughed at Regina's dramatic account, and I told her it beat going to fat camp. She agreed and told me she might meet some hot college guy, and then the summer would not be a total waste. I gave her one final hug and ran before her parents decided to interrogate me about my future.

The next stop was Janet's house. She was not at home. She was probably at one of her parents' restaurants having a family get-together. Unfortunately, I knew I would be forced to do something I hated, write her a good-bye letter. I hated writing good-bye letters. I'd much rather say good-bye than write it out. I decided I'd try to call her as soon as I thought she would be at home again.

The last stop was Jackie's house. My dad pulled up to her never-ending driveway, and I got out of the car and knocked on her door. Her mom opened the door with a huge smile on her face. "Hi, honey. How are you? I saw you today! You looked so cute in your cap and gown," she said. "Jackie is over her boyfriend's house. I know, I can't believe it either. She has a real boyfriend! They just left a few minutes ago. We all went out to dinner, and then Jackie and Ricky wanted to go to the movies so his parents dropped them off. Do you know Ricky? He is a football player, such a cute little boy."

I stood and looked at her in amazement. Jackie had a boyfriend, and not only did she have a boyfriend she had Ricky Johnson, the school's quarterback? What in the world was happening, and why didn't I know about it? I gave Jackie's mom a hug and headed to my dad's car. One more phone call I had to make tonight because I refused to write a letter.

I tried to reach both Jackie and Janet later that night, but neither of them were at home, so I gave up and decided I'd have to write them each a very brief good-bye letter once I got to camp.

Chapter 10

Big Girls Don't Cry

*I'm a big girl, no, not tall,
I mean round, rotund, and wide
When I walk the earth shakes and quakes
Sleeping earth forms wake
I don't like being fat, but the truth is food is a friend
and its comfort knows no end
I hold it dear, but pound for pound it leaves its mark
I guess it's time I learned to control the urge
As I shovel it in my mouth in copious loads
Society is not appreciative of my BMI, so I guess it's time
I march to my fate, a life filled with
tasteless salads and protein shakes!*

—*Fatima*

J. W. Hoffman

The dreaded day had come, my departure for fat camp. My parents dropped me off at the airport and tried to kiss me good-bye. I refused to kiss them; I felt that they were traitors sending me off to some forsaken camp in NC in order to make me over into some skinny person. OK, so I broke down and gave them hugs. After all, I had never been away from home for ten whole weeks before, and deep down I was a little scared. My mom as usual was crying, and kept saying, "Fatima baby, we're doing this for your health, you are beautiful just the way you are, but we want you to be beautiful and healthy." She squeezed most of the fat out of me with her hug, and she kissed me like I was a newborn baby again. Finally, I had to pull away from her to keep my dignity in tack as people stared at us in the airport. My dad, hugged me tight, and told me how proud of me he was, and that I could do anything I set my mind to do. That's just it, my mind didn't want to go, and I was set on staying home. However, my pleas and cries of abandonment went unheard, and my parents with their gate passes in hand walked me to my seat to wait until it was time for me to board the plane. They promised to stay there with me until the plane took off. Time went by quickly, and before you know it my flight number was called. I waved my final goodbyes to my parents, and I tried to prepare my mind for my fate at the stinking fat camp.

I boarded the plane, and the flight attendant who was in charge of my well-being, although a little overbearing, made sure that I had everything I needed. I mean, I knew of elementary-school students who had flown by themselves before. Why was she sweating me? I tried to take a nap, but the drone of the plane would not let me rest. So I pulled out *Marie Claire* instead and started critiquing the starving models. Before I knew it, I heard the monotone voice of the pilot announcing our landing. I looked out at the landscape, and all I could see for miles were mountains and trees. We definitely were not in Richmond anymore.

I got off the plane and started looking for the spot where I was supposed to meet the camp counselor who was picking me up. I found my place and saw a skinny white guy holding a sign saying "Mount Clear Fitness Camp and Retreat." I also spotted several other kids reluctantly walking up to the skinny guy. They looked just as happy to be there as I was. I carried my small suitcase and day bag over to the skinny guy and waited for him to acknowledge the group of chunky kids approaching him.

"Wow, what a group," he said. "I am so glad to have you all here. You are about to have the best camp experience of your lives at Mount Clear Fitness Camp and Retreat, where our slogan is 'Healthiness inside and out from the heart and soul.'"

I literary thought I was going to cough up the mixed nuts and Coke that the flight attendant had forced on me during the flight. He sounded straight like an advertisement. He ushered me and the other seven kids inside a neon-colored minivan decked out in the camp's logo from the interior to the exterior.

I sat in the very back, trying to make sure that no one would strike up a dreaded conversation with me. However, to my luck, a tall girl bigger than me came and sat so close to me that I could smell her warm Dorito breath. I figured she was like me and had hidden a bunch of snacks in some extra-hard-to-find places. I had stuffed my suitcase lining with Skittles, Airheads, Tootsie rolls, and Blow pops. I stuffed small bag of chips and snack size cookies inside the zippered sections of my bag as well. "Hey, my name is Lizzy. What's your name?" she asked with a big grin on her face.

"My name is Fatima," I said, dully and without further conversation.

"Cool, I've never heard of a name like that before. F-a-t-i-m-a, is that how you spell it? Anyway, I am not at all excited about this dumb camp. I am going to miss basketball camp this summer all because my dad thinks I would be a better player if I lose weight. He knows that I can run up and down the court with the best of them and shoot hoops like Jordan. But no, it's not enough. I have to fit in with the other hungry-looking girls on the team in my cute little shorts. Whatev.

"I am so over it all. On the way here I crammed so many chips, cookies, and chocolate bars down my throat I thought I would puke. I figured I better get it out of my system because the brochure says they will check you for everything."

When she finally stopped talking long enough to breathe, I thought about how I would have to throw out all of my delicious treats before they searched my bag, my stomach growled at the thought of it. I was so busy thinking about my snacks, that I didn't notice that everyone else was starting to get off the van. Lizzy was shaking my arm saying, "Girl, come on. It's time to get off."

I hated to admit it, but the scenery was absolutely beautiful. There were grassy hills and rows of colorful flowers and plants everywhere. The scenic mountain in the background was picturesque. Not that I was a nature person at all, but I could stop and admire it every now and then. The one thought in my mind though was that I was not looking forward to those hills at all.

We had to check in, so my new self-appointed best friend Lizzy and I stood in the long line waiting for our names to be called. While we were waiting, I took in all the campers. Some of them appeared to be just as bored with the entire process as me; other ones seemed to be scared out of their minds. There were about fifty of us in all, of various ages, colors, and shapes. Some of the guys looked cute; some of the girls would be supermodel material once they shed some pounds. Some of them would need an extra summer-camp experience to help them get into shape. I wondered what category I fell in. I really didn't see anyone in the crowd that I would click with, so I figured the hyper girl you knew was better than the people you didn't know, so I decided that Lizzy would have to do as my one true friend for the summer.

They finally called my name. I had to give them my luggage so they could rummage through it and check to see if I had any hidden treats in it. The whole process was a bit intrusive, and I was so glad when it was over. I had thrown out my secret stage of goodies as soon as I got off the bus in the trash can in the bathroom; I didn't want to be humiliated by a bunch of healthy fanatics going through my stash. Several other campers were not so lucky; they were hurt and embarrassed as their prize possessions of candy bars, chips, and cookies were thrown into the garbage.

Next was my weigh-in. I hated scales, and I rarely got on one. But it was time I faced my archnemesis, the scale. I was shocked to see how fat I really was. I mean, I was five foot seven, a bit tall for a girl, so the 235 pounds that the scale said I weighed didn't actually look as bad on me as it would have on a girl who was five feet tall. However, I still was considered a lumpy, rotund bundle of blubber to all of society.

After the shameful weigh-in and search and seizures, we were shown to our rooms according to our ages and weights. I decided to request Lizzy for a roommate. I mean, the fat girl you kinda knew was better than the fat girl you didn't. The rooms were the size of my walk-in closet, and the mattresses on the beds were so thin I could see the wooden boards under them. I could tell that this was going to be one of the best summers of my life.

Chapter 11

Day by Day

Day by day
It seems to me
That I am discovering a new way to be
I complained at first
Mumbled and grumbled
Though I'm still not thrilled
I discovered
I'm stronger
A small part of me has to admit
I've been giving a determination
I won't quit!

—Fatima

Finding Fatima

After about two weeks I eventually got into the routine at camp.

We woke up at 6:00, ran a mile, showered, and then ate a lovely breakfast at 7:00, which consisted of wheat toast, eggs, two slices of turkey bacon, and one fruit, with skim milk or water as our choices of beverages.

From 8:00 to 10:00, we had aerobics classes. The only good thing about these was that we could sign up for the classes we wanted. I enjoyed the cool music of the Zumba dance class. I figured I would be a full-fledged Spanish dancer by the time I was finished. Deep down I was hoping that one day Jorge would appreciate my dancing skills.

From 10:00 to 11:00, we had shower time again and a break before lunch.

Lunch was served at 12:00; it consisted of a small salad, grilled fish or chicken, a wheat roll, and our choice of fruit. I was practically starving at this camp, and no one seemed to care. The food was so flavorless I almost couldn't bare to eat it. I tried to pretend that it was Granny G's homemade soul food each time I took a bite of the tasteless crap, but even my imagination was not that good.

After lunch we had free time for about three hours.

At 4:00 we had to work out for about an hour in the gym. Then we had to shower and get ready for dinner.

At least I can say I was very clean this summer. At home during the summertime I usually didn't get out of my bed until 12:00, unless my mother harassed me. Speaking of my mom and dad, the first two weeks I was not allowed to talk to them. They wanted me to fully immerse myself in the camp routine without any interruptions. I took the time to write each of the Misfit crew at home, to tell them to pray for me that I wouldn't starve to death at the awful camp, and I wanted to guilt them into writing me back.

After my two weeks was up I talked to my parents about once a day. I tried to guilt my dad into letting me come home by telling him about my starvation and horror stories of the fitness regime, but he just laughed it off, telling me how proud he was of his baby girl for getting healthier. My mom kept saying over and over again how excited she was about the "fitness camp," and that she could not wait to take me shopping for my new clothes for my high-school career. I, on the other hand, could wait for eternity. I must admit that I was shedding weight like a cat sheds its fur. But I really didn't like being monitored every day like a small kid. I was looking forward to meeting my goal weight, set by the dietician so that I could get a free day from the strict regime at the camp.

One of the worst parts of having to attend the camp was the group counseling sessions. We were a bunch of fat kids in a huge group explaining why we loved food so much while a licensed therapist picked our words apart to see if we needed private sessions. When it was time for me to share, I tried to be as upbeat as possible. I didn't want to run the risk of actually having to do a private session. When it was my time to speak I just talked about how important it was to love yourself, and be healthy. What I really wanted to say was that in the world we lived in, being thin and pretty was more important than being happy or healthy. I mean from magazines, television shows, to models walking the runway, being beautiful seemed to be so important. The truth is the average woman was not a size two, and yet society loved those images. Plastic surgeons were rich, they make millions off of cutting, implanting, and injecting women to make the perfect female face and body. It's all so stupid to me, and I never want to become some skinny uptight superficial idiot, even if I am starting to like the idea of losing the weight. I seemed to have more energy, and I could actually run without stopping to take a breath every other second, but I never wanted to be thin! Never!

Lizzy proved to be an entertaining choice of roommates, and I found out that, although she was a serious basketball player, she was still a girly girl as well. One huge thing we had in common was that we both were a bit boy crazy. We both had similar tastes in guys. I liked tall guys with medium builds, meaning they had to have some type of visible muscle. I know right, a fat girl who likes buff guys, crazy huh? Lizzy and I were a bit hypocritical in our crushes. We were not big on the camp guys. We had our eyes on the extrafine camp counselors. There were ten male camp counselors, and out of ten of them there were about four of them that were

Finding Fatima

HOT! We narrowed our picks down to four guys, and we made ourselves a promise that by the end of camp one of us would get the guts and reveal her crush to the guy that she chose. We made a rule that all four guys were open game, and that whoever got to one of them first would win. We didn't really have a prize in mind, just serious bragging rights. Lizzy was already one step ahead of me because she was very confident around guys, and she didn't mind playing anybody one-on-one in basketball.

We came up with neat names to call them so that no one would know who we had crushes on in the camp. For instance, Justin, a tall black guy who looked like the singer Tyrese, was named Motions, because he always seemed to be using his hands in these crazy jerky movements whenever he spoke.

Adam—a tan, blond-haired, and blue-eyed surfer-like guy—was named Red Shirt, because he always seemed to wear the same red shirt every day, and no, it did not have camp logo on it. It was Nike all the way. I'm sure he took baths though, because the few times I was fortunate enough to get close to him, he smelled really good.

Jason was the next guy on our list of crushes. He was Asian, and he was like a Bruce Lee dream. We called him Tae Kwon Do, because he was always trying to get us to sign up to take his classes.

Nick was an Italian, and he reminded me of my school crush, Jorge, and my oldest crush Antonio Banderas. We called him Caliente, because he was truly the hottest guy at the camp. We knew this to be accurate because all the girl counselors hung around him like love-sick puppies begging him to look in their direction.

Deep down I thought Lizzy would probably win the bet, because she was really outgoing, and I was way too shy.

Chapter 12

Liberty

*I feel excitement running through my veins
No routine, no place to be
I can choose for once my own destiny
Choices, choices, choices
Lay before my eyes
I look up and then I decide
I will face my fears head-on today
So what if the cuteness of a boy happened to pave the way?*

—FATIMA

Finding Fatima

For the first time since I had arrived at the depressing and bodily destructive fat camp, I woke up with a grin on my face. I had finally done it; I had earned my free day. After six weeks at camp I had lost a total of twenty-five pounds. I was getting closer to my goal weight each day, and with four more weeks to go, I was ready for the entire experience to be over already. I was glad I didn't have to get up with the other girls that morning.

Unfortunately, Lizzy had not met her goal weight this time, so I would be spending my free day alone. I wasn't exactly sure how I was going to spend it, but I knew that I was going to lay in my makeshift bed as long as possible. The early schedule of waking up and working out had definitely affected me. I now hated the sound of alarm clocks, because I am not a morning person, especially during the summer. I was half asleep most of them time until our instructor started yelling or playing some loud music.

I finally decided to get up and get dressed at about 10:00. It was no biggie that I had missed breakfast, it wasn't like they were serving pancakes and sausage. I grabbed a Nutri-Grain bar from the vending machine and decided to go check out the free-day list-of-activities sign-up sheet. The activities listed were a matinee at a movie theater in town, a rowing trip, a zip-lining event, and water skiing. I know that it sounds a bit fickle, but I chose my activity based on the camp counselor. Yes, you can guess I wanted to be wherever Nick was, even if it meant getting way up in the air and tackling my fear of heights. I was about to defeat zip lining.

I decided to skip eating the Nutri-Grain bar; I needed an empty stomach if I was going to face my fear. The camp dietician would yell at me for it—she daily professed that breakfast was the most important meal of the day to get your metabolism going. I wasn't worried about my metabolism; I just didn't want to throw up on anyone.

I found the camp group that would be riding with me to the zip-line activity, and we waited for everyone to arrive before piling into the activity van. Nick jumped into the front seat of the van, turned around and looked at us, and said, "*Ciao amici*, are you ready for some fun today? This is the party van. Anybody that is not ready to par-TAY needs to head back to camp now."

All of the girls looked at him with love and adoration, while the guys just laughed and played along, chanting "Par-tay!" in goofy voices. I was so happy to have a free day I even started chanting the corny line.

We headed down the road and drove about thirty minutes out to the zip-line site. My stomach was turning in fifty different directions at the thought of getting forty feet in the air and swinging on a cable wire down a line for about a mile over a river. I just hoped the line wouldn't break. At the back of my mind I was still thinking about the bet I had made, and I knew that it may not happen that day. After all, I was sure Nick wouldn't want to kiss a girl who had just thrown up pure stomach acid.

Once at the site we listened to the instructor go over the rules and guidelines. Then, one by one, I watched my fellow campers get in the harness, which I must say was not attractive if you were carrying a few extra pounds. Finally, it was my turn.

Nick stood on the side cheering as we all zip lined. He had gone first in order to show us that it wasn't anything to be afraid of and how much fun it was. My eyes had been glued to his muscular build and handsome face the entire time. Now, he was standing calling my name with a huge grin on his face. I wanted to make him proud. So I threw caution to the wind and went for it.

At first terror filled me. I kept imagining the line breaking and me falling into the water and breaking every bone in my body. Then I decided to close my eyes and just hold on for dear life. I felt like a bird soaring in the sky; it was over so quickly I almost—and I mean almost—wanted to do it again. Nick was waiting on the other side. He grabbed me and gave me a big hug, and said, "I knew you could do it, Fatima. I am so proud of you." I clung to him enjoying every moment of the hug so much so that he had to pull away. I reluctantly let him go.

After the zip-line experience some of the other campers decided to try bungee jumping. I, on the other hand, had had enough adventure

Finding Fatima

for the day. Nick and the other counselors gave us the option of bungee jumping or eating lunch early, and I decided to go with lunch. Of course the camp's dietitian and resident cook had made us a tasteless lunch of a tuna-salad sandwich, fruit salad, one tomato, and a bottled water. I sat beside Nick and three other campers at a picnic table to eat my lunch.

Nick started asking us questions about school and what we did for fun. The two guys in the group, whose names were John and Richard, started talking about all this technical computer stuff they did, while Judy, the other girl in the group, expounded upon her huge collection of rare stones. I decided to keep my boring hobbies to myself, but everyone insisted I share them with the group. I told them I liked to read, act in school plays, and write poetry. They begged me to share a poem, and I told them I didn't share my poetry. I was happy when the subject changed to our favorite movies and actors/actresses.

After lunch, Nick decided to take us hiking up a large hillside. Not one for hiking, I forced myself to go just to be near him. Surprisingly, he walked side by side with me while the other campers trudged ahead of us at a steady pace. I tried not to show how hard I was breathing as Nick starting asking me questions.

"Fatima, how old are you?"

I told him I was fourteen, and going to the ninth grade.

"You are very mature for a fourteen-year-old. I'm only sixteen, but I probably act like a twelve-year-old compared to you," he jokingly said. I just stared at him in awe. I didn't want to ruin the moment of a hot guy talking to me, so I just looked into his eyes and listened intently.

Nick continued, "I try not to take myself too serious. You know I came to this camp four years ago because my parents told me I was starting to look like the Goodyear Blimp. At first I hated everything about it, but then I started seeing how important it is to be healthy. Some of the people in my family are overweight because we, Italians love to eat. Not my parents though. They are very into their appearance and could not stand having a chunky son, not when their daughter is on her way to becoming a supermodel. She of course is off the hook, because she promised to be the face of the business's new lean Italian frozen dinners. The advertising department came up with a corny line: 'We Italians love to eat, but we also love to look good,'" Nick said.

I could not help agreeing with him on how corny the slogan was. I mean, I could've thought of something better than that myself.

Nick kept on talking, and I wasn't about to interrupt. He said, "Just in case you were wondering, I'm kind of the outcast in my family. I refuse to go to school for business so that I can take over the family restaurant chains and make them even more money. Everyone in my family spends their time talking about their portfolios and how much they're worth. I find it all materialistic and sad, being that most of the people in the world are struggling to make it. While we live in a ridiculous five-thousand-square-foot home with just four people in it—well, really three if you don't count my sister, who is never home."

I decided to respond for the first time since the conversation started. "Wow, I thought I was the only one with social issues about having money in a world of poor people, but your family really has money. My family would probably seem like a welfare case compared to them," I jokingly told him.

He laughed at me and said, "I know I'm going to sound like a poor little rich boy preaching to the choir, but I want my life to mean something. I want to do more than just earn a bank account. I want to be a pediatrician, travel the world, and help children who really need it," Nick said.

"I think it's great that you have a plan for your life, and no, it's not cheesy or preachy. It's actually cool. At least you have a plan," I told him.

"As smart as you seem, I know that you probably have a lifetime plan in place yourself," Nick said.

I laughed at him and told him I didn't have a clue about what I was going to be. I was still finding myself.

He laughed and said "You're not alone. An occupation is not a label of who we are; it's just a job that we decide we want to do. Who we are takes years to discover."

I was deeply and completely in love at this point. I couldn't believe that a guy like him existed. I mean, he was superhot, sensitive, caring, and had dreams of actually helping people. I'm sure he could run for office and win in a matter of seconds. He would be the first decent politician in the world. I had to find out if he was a real person or my dream boy in ghost form, so I did something crazy. I pinched his arm.

He rubbed his arm and asked, "Hey, what did I do?"

I responded, "I just wanted to check and see if you were real or not, because for a minute there you were sounding too good to be true."

He looked at me for a long time and then said, "I don't exactly need to pinch you to see if you're real, but I wouldn't mind testing the theory in another way," he said looking at my lips.

I'm not sure it's possible for me to blush, but if I was I'm sure I turned ten shades of red. I probably looked like my grandpa when he stayed in the sun too long and got what he called his "summer farmer tan," but mine was all in my face. I decided to take the conversation to more safe territory and asked him how he liked working at the camp.

Nick said, "I work here every summer to escape the restaurant madness. I love the fact that they have a day camp for children with special needs, and of course I get to work with you all as well," he said with a ridiculous smile that nearly melted all the extra fat from my body.

I was about to propose to this man and totally embarrass myself. All I could think was why was he talking to me of all the girls at camp; he could have chosen anybody else. He couldn't possibly like a self-centered, introverted Debbie Downer like myself. But he just kept right on talking to me and asking me questions for the entire hike. I hung on his every word, and when he asked me something I tried to sound halfway intelligent in my reply.

Finally, when we reached the camp, everyone decided they didn't want the fun to end, so someone came up with the idea of us all roasting marshmallows over the campfire. I was psyched. Any opportunity to spend more time with Nick was all I needed. I ran back to my cabin, took a quick shower to wash away the grime of the day, sprayed perfume on myself, and grabbed a blanket. I tried to locate my girl Lizzy, but she was nowhere to be found. I assumed she was somewhere trying to win the bet, but I refused to go out without a fight. It was my night.

Chapter 13

Lips

*Funny we all have them just below our
noses and above our chins
But have you ever considered their purpose?
One day I did
I discovered their joy and felt their bliss
In a simple dance, a small feathery kiss*

—FATIMA

We all gathered around the huge campfire with our blankets and marshmallows. I almost shed a tear for the absence of my delicious s'mores, but I was content as could be because Nick asked to sit right next to me on my blanket. I couldn't move over fast enough for him to sit down. We started talking about music and how it had changed over time.

"You know, I must be an old soul because I still like people like Marvin Gaye, Otis Redding, and Al Green. My parents still have an old record player, so one night I go downstairs to the basement, dust the records off, put them on one by one, and I just started grooving. But I know you don't even know what I'm talking about; you're probably too young," Nick said.

I started to laugh, because my Granny G kept a collection of old records as well, and in addition to her gospel greats she had the old school "Let's Get It On" crew as well.

Nick and I both broke out singing "Let's Get It On." It got a bit awkward because Nick and I just started staring at each other in the middle of the song. I knew right then I had to act fast, so I made the excuse of us needing to go back to camp to get more blankets because everyone kept complaining about the cold night air, and I asked him to walk back with me to the cabins. Crazy thing is, when we started walking, both of us went in the opposite direction of the cabins, and we simultaneously reached for each other's hands. Once we were far away from the camp members, we just held hands in silence for a while, and then Nick said, "Look, Fatima, I never ever crush on a camper. I have strict rules I follow when it comes to my job, and I take them very seriously…but there is something about you. I just feel so drawn to you. I feel like I've known you forever, and I've only talked to you today. I think you are feeling the same way, or at least I hope you are."

I looked up at him then and nodded my head up and down like a bobblehead in agreement. My lips were tingling and doing all kinds of weird things. I knew it was about to happen, my first kiss, so I leaned into his muscular frame and closed my eyes and primped my lips like you do when you are making the duck face.

Finding Fatima

He grabbed my face between his hands and said, "I want to look you in the eyes when I kiss you."

I opened my eyes and looked into his and was completely lost. The kiss was so tender and sweet, and yet I could feel tiny prickles of sensation flowing from my lips down to my toes. I wanted it to go on forever, but then we both heard voices coming closer and closer toward us, so we reluctantly pulled apart.

"Hey, I wonder what's taking Nick and Fatima so long," we heard someone say. I realized it was Justin.

"I don't know man, but from the way they were singing to each other back there, they may have decided to get it on, hahaha," came the response from Jason.

"Yeah, you funny. You know Nick would never go for a fatso, even if she has dropped a few pounds. Most mixed chicks are hot, but wow, I couldn't get down with her."

"Man, shut up. Fatima is a sweet girl. She's worth her extra weight. I might even holler."

I felt like balling up and cringing inside. Justin was making fat jokes. At least Jason was taking up for me, if you could call it that. As for Nick, I was so embarrassed I couldn't even look at him. He tried to grab my arm, but I just wanted to run and hide, so that's what I did. I ran as fast as I could back to the camp. I probably broke a camp record or two, but in my state of anger I couldn't have cared less. It was one thing to admit to myself that I was a fatty; it was entirely different to hear two of my crushes saying it out loud.

Once inside my cabin, I let my tears fall freely and without restraint. How could such a sweet memory be so messed up with ugly words? I guessed that was my fate. Then, my mind starting asking all sorts of questions. Did Nick really like me? Or was I just some fat girl to get some loving from? I didn't know, and part of me never wanted to find out.

Chapter 14

The Blues

*I don't have no horn to play a mournful tune
I don't have no sultry voice to sing my pain through
I can't find a note to move you up or down, all I got,
All I got
Is my feelings congested in my chest, crushing
my heart, and choking my neck
I thought love was real, but I see it's an illusion
Cloudy pillows of smoke that disappear in a blink
So who needs a heart? My conclusion is this
Love stinks!*

—F*ATIMA*

Finding Fatima

I spent the next week in total depression and loneliness. Lizzy spent every moment she could with her new jock boyfriend—yes, boyfriend. She had met a local baller who happened to be just as good as she was. They had fallen madly in love in a matter of seconds apparently. They spent every free moment she had together, either playing basketball or making out. I just could not build up the confidence or courage to approach Nick about the kiss. Instead I just pretended like it never happened. Nick did the same, so nothing ever got resolved.

I decided to work out even harder; I decided to use Justin and Jason's words as motivation. I deliberately chose activities that kept me away from Nick. I also made sure to stay as far away from Justin and Jason as possible. I didn't want to have to fight two muscular teenage boys. I could not stomach their fake concern for my weight lost, or at least Justin's fake concern. Jason did seem like a pretty decent guy.

I built up this grand story in my head to figure out why Nick had kissed me. I decided it was a joke, or to make fun of me in some way. It sounded crazy, but the fat girl in me could not understand how a hot guy like him surrounded by tall, skinny blond girls and shapely African American queen coworkers could really want a mixed, chunky, nappy-headed, green-eyed fatty. Yes, pretty harsh, but that's how I saw myself in comparison to the other girls at the camp.

I got another free day because of all my hard work, and instead of signing up for some extra-risky camp activity like I had done last time, I decided to take in a movie. I walked in the theater feeling nervous. I though my stomach would growl hungrily when I smelled the buttery popcorn, but the funny thing is, it didn't even gurgle one time. I decided that this health kick had finally started to work. I didn't even care what movie was playing; I chose some cheesy comedy. I just wanted to lose myself in the empty theater. No one ever signed up for movies on free days except for the couples who wanted to use the dark theater for their own purposes.

I was finally starting to get into the movie when I thought I heard someone calling my name from behind. "Fatima, Fatima." I recognized the voice, and yet I was afraid to believe it could be him. I turned around and saw Nick walking toward me.

"Look, Fatima, you've been ignoring me for the past week, and in a few weeks camp will be over and you'll have to leave. I have to talk to you, and it can't wait. So excuse the fact that I stalked you and followed you to the theater and please let me escort you outside for a much-needed talk," Nick said.

I looked around the empty theater to make sure no one was interested in our drama and decided there was no better place for a heart-to-heart than the local theater. I got up and followed him outside. But I refused to let him talk first. I had to let him know what I was feeling, and I was not going to hold back anything.

"Nick, I don't have much to say to a fake guy who pretends to be some great humanitarian and then turns out to be a huge jerk. After your friends said those words, all I could think of was, 'Why would this hot, smart guy want me, a fat, unattractive girl, when he could have anyone else in the world? I'm really not a great catch.' So, I figured maybe you didn't want me, maybe it was a game, or just some experiment to see how far I would let you go. I don't know. At any rate, I guess I should thank you for my first kiss. Even if it was all a big lie, it probably would have never happened if it wasn't for you. I mean, you can't help that one of your friends is a total jerk, and the other one is a semi-jerk, can you?

Nick angrily said, "Fatima, I realize that you don't know me that well. If you did truly know me, you would know that I don't believe in playing games. I've been where you are. I've been made fun of, and I know how it feels. I don't want some stick-like girl whose only concern is how pretty she looks at all times. I want someone I can laugh with, talk to, and be my corny self around.

"Justin is an idiot who only comes here to pick up girls. If you had stayed around instead of running away, you would have heard the way I laid into him for disrespecting you, I almost had to reach out and touch him, as peaceful as I am. Jason is my friend, and he is a pretty good guy.

He apologized and agreed that you are quite a catch and even said if I wasn't interested then he would be.

"No matter what they think, though. Your value and self-worth can't be based on what people see or think of you. It has to be from someplace deeper. I think that God made you perfectly and beautifully, and that's why I kissed you then, and that's why I want to kiss you now."

Let's just say my second kiss had more fireworks than my first. We didn't stop to breathe.

Chapter 15

Saying Good-bye

I refuse to say the words that would bring this dance to an end
I found in weeks a forever, loving friend
A check to my mate, a kindred being
He is my joy, and I am his
So instead of good-bye
Let us both try to always remember this one thing
True spirits touching never truly end, so I bid you not good-bye
I just say, "Until we meet again!"

—F<small>ATIMA</small>

Unfortunately, the next few weeks went by in a blur. I lost weight without trying because I spent every moment I could with Nick, hiking, biking, and boating. We stole kisses in between our excursions; we became so good at hiding our affection for each other in the presence of the other camp members that it almost became a secret game to us. Of course we knew that everyone was aware we were an item. We just made sure the instructors stayed in the dark. They were the ones we had to really watch out for. We invented special hand signals and code words when we wanted to sneak off and be alone without being noticed.

Lizzy was so happy when she found out about Nick and me. She made me a queen for the day T-shirt, to celebrate me winning our bet. I mean I was the only one to end up with one of the hot counselors, but I no longer considered Justin or Jason hot. Lizzy suggested we start double-dating so we could hang out before camp ended, so our twosome became a group of four. We refused to even try to play them in a game of basketball, but we sure kicked their buts in canoeing all day, every day. I had never in my life had so much fun and freedom, and I didn't want it to end. But it did. The last day of camp we were having a big party to celebrate achieving our weight goals. I wanted Nick to see me in something other than some shorts and a T-shirt, so me and Lizzy set out to find dresses that accentuated our new weight loss and still made us look superhot.

After we both had tried on about a dozen or so dresses that all seemed to be the wrong size, (meaning for the first time in my life something was too big for me) Lizzy chose a red-and-white floral wrap dress that looked really good on her tall frame, and I found a lacey, white sleeveless dress with a belted green ribbon that Lizzy swore matched my eyes.

Lizzy spent about two hours trying to straighten my hair out, and to my amazement it actually worked. We decided to skip the makeup, because we both didn't own anything besides your minimum lip gloss and mascara, and we refused to go around begging for such personal items.

We made the guys meet us at the dance because we wanted to surprise them with our makeovers. We practically skipped hand in hand to the dance hall, a.k.a. the commons area. I must admit, the counselors had done a great job transforming the sterile place into an island dream; we barely recognized the place.

Once inside, we spotted our men, and they spotted us. I was not prepared for the look on Nick's face; it was a cross between adoration and some other glossy-eyed emotion I couldn't name. He ran up to me and stuttered about how great I looked. His exact words were, "Fatima you look beautiful!"

Lizzy and I both seemed to be the center of attention for some crazy reason because it seemed like everybody was staring at us. Some girls we didn't even know demanded we tell them where we brought our dresses and where we had gotten our makeovers done. We told them we had went to some random store in the mall, and that we hadn't had makeovers. They looked at us as if we were lying and abruptly walked away.

We danced all night, because one thing I can do very well was move on a dance floor. Nick was trying to do some kind of Salsa dance, but I had to bring him up to speed on the more popular dances of our times. He just shook his head and watched as me and Lizzy ruled the dance floor. Not to be outdone, when they played the slow music, I almost melted on the dance floor. Nick's moves were smooth and sultry enough to make me forget where I was for a second.

We ended the night with a long, sweet kiss and promises that we would never forget how great it was. Deep down I knew I had to prepare myself to say good-bye. I could feel the tears already forming in my eyes.

The next day, everybody at the camp was surprised because, when we woke up, the first thing we saw in our commons area was parents everywhere waiting to see their kids. I was under the impression that I would be flying back just as I had come: solo. But nope, my mom and dad were among the parents trying to find their newly slim daughter among children of different sizes and ages.

I found them first and tapped my dad on the shoulder. "Oh my gosh, baby girl, you look awesome," he said as he picked me up in a bear hug.

"Put me down, Dad. This is so embarrassing," I mumbled under my breath.

My mom started crying like a baby. "Oh, Fatima, my beautiful Fatima, I missed you so much. You've changed so much. You're even prettier now." I begged her to stop crying, and once she did I gave her a hug.

I saw Nick standing in the back watching the entire reunion unfold, and I motioned for him to come over. I wanted him to meet my parents, because who knew? Maybe one day he would be their son-in-law. My dad almost crushed his hand while shaking it, and my mom couldn't stop staring at him because he was "such a cute boy."

I gave them my bags to put in the car in order to keep them busy. I said my tearful good-byes to Lizzy, and we both promised to visit each other and keep in touch. Then, I prepared myself to say good-bye to Nick. We had been discussing our good-byes for the past few weeks, how we would call, facetime, text, and try to come see each other as much as possible. We had decided we wouldn't say good-bye, just "see ya later."

He gave me a big bear hug, and I squeezed him and smelled his addictive scent, trying to program it to memory. I didn't know what brand of cologne he wore, but he smelled masculine yet sweet at the same time. We reluctantly let go of each other and kissed and said in unison, "See you later!"

Epilogue

Just Me

*So what can I say? I'm still me, but I
guess the outside has changed
No longer living in a bubble
Yeah, I'm still discovering
who I want to be
I found love, friends, and hopefully
the true and real me
But I'm not worried or scared, like my Granny G says
God always has a purpose and a plan
So my life is really just starting, and I'm
looking ahead and with each new day
I hope to be more and more free
of stress, doubt, and insecurities
I hope to live instead in peace, love, and joy
I'm closing one chapter of my life and opening a new door
What awaits? I don't know…
But for once in my life, without a doubt
I'm not afraid to find out…*

—F*atima*

Made in the USA
Lexington, KY
18 August 2018